EACH LEAF

SHINES SEPARATE

4

Each Leaf
Shines Separate

Rosanna Warren

POEMS

W. W. Norton & Company

NEW YORK / LONDON

Published simultaneously in Canada by Stoddart,
a subsidiary of General Publishing Co. Ltd, Don Mills, Ontario.
Printed in the United States of America.
First Edition
Library of Congress Cataloging in Publication Data
Warren, Rosanna.
Each leaf shines separate.
I. Title.
PS3573.A7793E2   1984   813'.54   84–8026

ISBN 0-393-01914-4
ISBN 0-393-30205-9 pbk.

W. W. Norton & Company, Inc., 500 Fifth Avenue, New York, N.Y. 10110
W. W. Norton & Company Ltd., 37 Great Russell Street, London WC1B 3NU

1 2 3 4 5 6 7 8 9 0

ACKNOWLEDGMENTS

Agni Review: "Orchard," "Invitation au Voyage: Baltimore" /
Antioch Review: "Echo" / Atlantic Monthly: "The Field," "Virgin
Pictured in Profile" / Chicago Review: "A Cypress," "Funere Mersit
Acerbo" / Crescent Review: "Knossos" (originally "Not the
Terraces") / Cumberland Review: "Wreckers: Coast of
Northumberland," "Embrace," "Jigsaw Puzzle in the Suburbs" /
Georgia Review: "Painting a Madonna" / The Nation: "Music for
Railroad, Telephone Wire, and Easter" / New England Review:
"Drowned Son," "Antietam Creek" / Partisan Review: "History as
Decoration" / Poet & Critic: "Snow" / Seneca Review: "Through the
East Door" (originally "Theora"), "Rocamadour," "In a Tuscan
Landscape," "Funerary Portraits" / Shenandoah: "Daylights,"
"Renoir" / Skyline: "Interior at Petworth: From Turner" / Southern
Review: "Snow Day," "Visitation" / Yale Review: "Illustrated
History," "Omalos," "To Max Jacob," "Alps" / "Pastorale" first
appeared in Homage to Robert Penn Warren, a collection of essays
edited by Frank Graziano, Logbridge-Rhodes, 1981. Several of
these poems have previously appeared in Snow Day, a chapbook,
published by Palaemon Press Limited in 1981. I would like to
thank Yaddo, The Ingram Merrill Foundation; and The Newton,
Massachusetts Arts Council for their support.

ILLUSTRATIONS

Heddi Vaughan Siebel, charcoal on paper, photographed by David Caras:
p. 1, Aquatic Plants (1983); p. 33, Eel (1983); p. 61, Aquarium Corner (1983).

To Stephen, Benjamin,

and Katherine

Contents

I

II

III

ONE

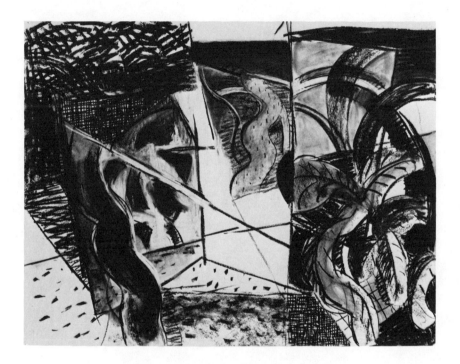

Garden

(Crete—New York)

I

Petals fell white and remorseless as
snow layering sleep on sleep as sky
hands unrolled one endless bolt of dimity, and down
all floated, veiling the garden where
the real gardenia once, from its cumbrous vase,
exploded in a sand-grit gust to shed
benediction on the sleeping cat:
made the old woman laugh as it unloosed
dangerous sweetness on the air.

II

We lie, one closed corolla of winter limbs.
The room breathes drowsy with the scent of white
from the window plant. Dredged from sleep,
he yawns, stretches, prowls for clothes.

III

To return to the first gardenia:
in a sea-wind,
shattered.
In a Cretan garden, stars
of jasmine pitched straight down a wall.
Beyond drugged leaves, the rock

3

hoisted sheer up one hundred yards above
thistle and olive tangle to
caverned galleries where
the villagers—May, '41—hid
from the shredded air, ten days.
That was the first invasion
conducted wholly from the sky.
The Germans stayed four years. The people took
to the rock.
But long ago, falling thick as centuries,
stone Turkish cannonballs had stunned
the land, and long
before that, the Mycenean spearheads drove
Minoans deep into their island's granite mind.

IV

The plant from Seventh Avenue
sits on the Ninth Street sill.
Leaves, at the florist's shining green,
cringe like small hands.
Aging, the flowers turn
mild butter yellow. But new buds twist
as pale green torches in the fists
of many liberties.
Light drawls in from the window,
delivers the room.
I rise from my sheets,

shake off my petals, veils of sleep,
water the potted gardenia from a jar.
It's morning. I begin.

I begin my life.

World Trade Center

We are so small beneath the stars
we figure as barely
visible *écriture:*
minute provisoes on the lease
the squinting lawyer can't make out.

Why don't you look at me, you say.

I look but you sit with your back to the window. There
reels the royal document of sky.
Below, in river blackness, a single tug-
boat drags one point of light across the dark.
It wants to punctuate
the entire, shiftless story of the night.
The water, invisible, slides.

We are so small beneath the stars,
we dance, the couples dance, flame fingers air
at each small table from a small glass cup.

We have not been consulted on these laws.

We dance, we look, I can't
read our own sentence,
our candle guttered in its pool of wax.
Outside the stars are wheeling. Bridges string
sequins from nowhere to nowhere. Jeweled words
lie tossed on the blackened scroll:

tossed to the curled, soiled fringes of the world.

Funerary Portraits

In a world of stone, they grieve in stone.

1 / *Mother*

The mother presses her head to her hand, already
bowing under the weight
of her strange childlessness, while the child
like the child still uncarved somewhere, reaches out
to the figure who sits, half-veiled,
dazed, with a small box on her lap
containing those objects—comb,
perfume vial, jade necklace—which she will take
with her to a world where they can no longer be used
and where beauty is not an issue.

2 / *Hunter*

His dogs would follow him. They are pure
energy pent in arabesques of tails,
curling spines, arched necks. But they are held
back by the small servant who knows
his master, this time, has no quarry.
In marble, they whine, and scratch. But he, the young
huntsman whose ordinary brow has
cleared suddenly and widened into something
like an ideal proportion, has no ear
for them. He listens, instead, to a new
chorus of voices, not animal, not
human, but as though
eucalyptus leaves sharpened each

other, blade scraping on blade, and
for the fulfillment of the ceremony, waited
only for him.

3 / *Timarista and Krito*

Her fingers on the girl's bare neck, light
and possessive, the girl's head lowered,
arm raised, chiton spilling like water
across uptilting breasts—if these two
are mother and daughter, how
erotic to have given birth, how
the young one—the live one—folds still further
toward the embrace, her silk in flight
from tiny clasps, while Timarista, the elder, stands
column-fluted, staring beyond
the whorls of Krito's
hair, ear, drapery, her past
pleasure knotted in this girl and now
released, so that she half-
turns, her free left arm
thrust out, away, hand open as though
to seize on a new life.

Illustrated History

(Crete 1977)

They erected habitations,
set boats on a certain sea, and quarried stone.
Peoples and peoples arrived.
Eventually, horses, and the arts of war.
It was thought that planting grass (unknown
in this clime) and layers
of rock, gravel, and tar under the sun
and making love, and wine, would shore up the town.

Swift shadows flecked the court.
Paint cracked on shutters.
The mulberry tree survived
the highway, and blunt pruning, with its own
empurpled knobs and brilliant, surly green.
Children played hopscotch in the toppled halls
trusting only the lines they drew.

Sea scumbled green frothlight on the sand
with rinds, bottles, oil. Cats ran the ruins.
The harbor leapt in the wind. Newspapers,
grease-stained, flared. Islands dissolved,
and palaces.
                    They left
brown bodies darting—quick cries of boys—
and then, in cobalt chalk-light, cries only.
Salt-glittering, the cries slashed blue
water as fish, flight-lifted, slice bright arcs in air.

9

Knossos

Most beautiful, under the stunning sun
among pine-scented cicadas,
lemon-olive shimmer and
noon-smashed rocks,

were not the terraces.
Not columns, courtyards, altars, halls;
not the queen's bath, horns of bulls,
fretwork sewers, flocks

of azure monkeys harvesting
frescoed papyrus over rainbow hills;
not fleets tallied on clay nor tall
men with helmets, bull's hide shields

and imperial hungers, but
the ribbed, light-hollowed bee through whose
shell the sun now shot
a labyrinth intaglioed with sky.

Omalos

The moon bloats full and white
with spider eggs tonight.
Furred in moonlight, the fat weed
waits and will welcome moon-sac birth
with broad thick leaves outspread.
Thistles point. Rocks
hunker into themselves.
There is a regularity in the *dangle-dang*
of goat bells, sheep bells, in the hills.
The night world leans.
To each sleeper, hunched into his dream
in his stone hut on the plain,
floats downward from rock jag, wavering,
the baleful laughter of goats.

Haoma

First, the omen of the dead fish.
They glittered along the weed line of the shore.
Two days later the sea retched up its gut.

We walk back alleys
where columbine fingers the Cyclopean wall,
where children keep picking an ancient quarrel apart.

There should be a speaker, iris-tongued,
to read the fish and the great water.

The rats die too. You see them lying
with cans, crushed jasmine, melon rinds.

The earth churns in its bones at night:
stars rocking, roof lines tilt.

Haoma: they say it's a tree
whose juice immortalized.
Haoma, haoma, we call for our gardens.
The wind halloos us and our syllables.

The spawned child
walks, won't speak,
paws for sea glass in the sea-drenched street.

There is no more work in the vineyards.
The grapes are gathered, crushed, in casks.
There is no more work in the vineyards.
The earth is charred.

Can you imagine one single love to endure?

Listen, the wind, it rises again.
Drugged with Asia, weighted with ocean passage,
it roils through the town and it respects no house,
no word, no window. Shutters crash. Red wind:

It's only the wind.

History as Decoration

Float over us, Florence, your banners
of assassination, your most expensive
reds: Brazil, Majorca lichen, cochineal.
Let the Neoplatonic Arno flow
crocus yellow. Let palazzo walls
flaunt quattrocento dyes: "little
monk" and "lion skin." We pay for beauty; beautiful
are gorgeous crimes we cannot feel—

they shone so long ago. And those philosophies
too pretty in spirit ever to be real.
City of fashion. Leonardo chose
the hanged Pazzi conspirator for a theme:
"Tawny cap; black satin vest," he wrote,
"black sleeveless coat, lined; turquoise
jacket lined with fox; Bernardo di
Bandino Baroncigli; black hose."

So dangled the elegant corpse, *bella figura*
though its tongue stuck out. The keen, gossipy
faces still peer from Ghirlandaio's walls
and from the streets we elbow through today.
History flashes in banknotes. Gold, jade, corals
twinkle from hand to hand, while the spectral glare
of Savonarola's sunset bonfire licks the square
and his cries ascend and blend with Vespers bells.

Daylights

So the sky wounded you, jagged at the heart,
glass shard flying from liquor store window smashed.
They had warned you, blue
means danger. The kid runs off
zigzagging the crowd, clutching his prize of Scotch;
the liquor man yells. Those Grecian dreams
endure even New York. You think
you're safe, humdrumming along
the sidewalk's common, readable gray,
calmly digesting your hunk of daily bread,
with flesh enough on your bones to cast some shade,
but puddle flashes, car window glints,
a stranger casts you a glance from a previous life:
the sky! And there you stand
unclouded, un-named, as naked as
the chosen Aztec facing the last shebang—
(*his* last shebang; the globe keeps rolling along
slipslop in its tide of blood)—

So there you stand
holding your sky-stabbed heart in your hands
to offer—to whom?—
while the liquor man curses the daylights
out of the cop, and the crowd
clumps dully away.
And you: "What *you* lookin' at?
Move on!" So you
move on and grateful, by God,
in the grit gray light of day.

Echo

I sit
in spackled light that sifts
from the high pines
while the sisters, my mother and aunt, talk
of how their father left
and the farm failed, and how
they rode the pony over the hill
but do not mention their mother
screaming;
                as the aging friend
watches, he remembers them running as girls,
tries to picture their strayed
daughters, sons, his own
wife lost in dismembering years; as light
pools gold in olive oil left on the plates
and Midas-like touches the pale green globes
of grapes and gleaming ellipse
at the rim of a glass;

gene by gene, the tiny transcriptions
continue. At night
I dream of a chain
of bodies, tawny in forest light,
gripped each to each by the hand,
wading across the muscled rills of a stream
that coils among jutted rocks before
plunging, blind, down
to the pool below.
                The house

peels back from its sleep
at a cry of pain. The cry
not mine. My mouth
is closed. My dead
grandmother stands at the top of the stairs,
lips wide, hair wild, as she stood
years back, and I, a child, stared at her there.
The cry she utters
is not hers, either. It is
its own echo down the long halls
and owns us all.

I reach out my hand, still damp
from the stream.
I open my mouth.

Snow

On Easter, snow fell
gently past branches,
joining the old, deep
white, and whether the
ground floated up to
the sky, or the sky
down, who could tell, it
happened so motion-
lessly, all we knew
was suspension in
blankness. Inside,
words fell, gently past
windows, past faces
in front of the windows,
"Why didn't you bring
more logs for the fire?"
"Wash your hands." The trees
stood written on snow,
snow written on trees,
I remembered his face
white, pained, yearning to
speak, and sweat beading.
He did not know then
he would die.
                    Meanwhile,
snow passed into snow,
the family massed
for dinner, the fire
spat, and all that day

I had not been out-
side. I had not yet
entered that white.

Alps

The mountains taught us speechlessness.
A snowshoe hare loped to its place

in silence, through powder. We spoke
only below, in the village, and then
of merely human absences, as when
G. departed, taken sick,

or when we had to conclude affairs
that had not been love, or even,
often, affairs—conclude them in
haste, with our hats on, there by the stairs:

for whatever they'd been, they had
at least composed the bleak-
ness. And hard enough it had been to speak
of those un-mountainous matters, in few words, without fraud.

A Cypress

I

There are some who,
having earth pressed into brain, eye sockets,
pit of stomach, cave of groin, believe
they will rise again
in more than stalk and bud.
That the crystal of soul
survives, and even communicates
with *confrères* still trapped in the old
unwieldy box of flesh.
And there are others who take this matter of dying
as a fine figure of return, a metaphor
in which Orpheus, Theseus, Christ, can dignify
a "highly lonely," a week's despondency, or a month in the
  bughouse.
They return from these putative hells
radiant, shedding glints of resurrection at every turn.

II

This is no figure, what you have done.
I do not see what light
flowers from buried flesh,
and torn limbs do not turn into musical notes
marked on the stave of pain.
You are conversing with no sages
in Elysian fields. You do not even feel

the rain, which has fallen steadily all this day
as though the sky were pouring itself completely out.
You did not smell
the dust as it rose from under the first, fat drops,
or hear the whispered, soothing "Sshh" with which the leaves
received the rain.
This is no figure, what you have done.

III

The sky is a soiled tarpaulin lashed
down over us, over the dim mass
of summer green.
This world, too hugely green, absorbs the rain
and stays absorbed in itself.
The sky is a tarpaulin lashed: it leaves
no way for crawling out.
And even you are planted here,
who seemed to choose otherwise,
in the grand terrarium and ritual
circulation.
The rain has found you out, though you do not
feel or know it. Lilac and rotting fishbait steep
in steaming air. Tomatoes swell
clammily on the vine. Too-vivid grass
exhales the rain back up to the low-slung sky.
But nothing sighs you back, and all your talk

of spirit communion is an emptiness
the rain and dank air seep to occupy.

IV

What a factory, your lungs, while you were alive.
So many secrets to confide,
orders to give, implausible notions and interpretations
to press out into an atmosphere
almost too heavy for this labor.
We did not always listen,
and, when we did, usually did not agree.
For a while, we will remember you, and manufacture
fables of our own, until we too
cease to obstruct the wind.

V

A tree
stands planted in no soil, but in mid-air
which is the bottom of the painting.
It never rains there, but a lemon sky
holds the tree upright.
Painted by a child, it is a cypress, emerald flame
erect on its wick of trunk.
And just above it, to the left,

23

the sun, in Chinese red, turns
a perpetual cartwheel with pronged spokes outright.

It is a lie, this continually
flickering and unearthly tree.
I pass it on
for its brave gaudiness, since our sky
still unlooses itself
and the oaks shuddering in their green shawls
are rooted inexorably in loam we all become.
I pass it on, by way of a goodbye,
which, though you cannot hear it, still will be
the first story in that collection of lies
we who still live in seasons
already compose for you.

Wreckers: Coast of Northumberland

(J. M. W. Turner)

What they save from the wreck
is indistinct, and the sea on the glistening sand
could just as well be sky. Or rather, three
elements, earth, water, and air, are seen to take

the properties of mist, and so dissolve.
The people themselves, as they haul junk from the waves,
seem a kind of dark, scriptural weed
destined, like the spars they grope for, to revolve

in tides endlessly turned back on themselves.
If they lured the ship, they are towed in turn
through foam by the shapes they save.
The sea lunges in from distant shelves

yawning for plunder, hurls itself at the shore
as bridal spray. A cloud
gapes its vast jaw over the ship
foundering on the horizon. Nothing more

can be saved from this scene. It is all
already lost, no sooner seen
than shrouded, the lucid brush
mingling, like the vague wreckers, possession and memorial.

25

The Field

(from Chagall)

The man is dreaming under a green field.
His legs have grown leagues-long in sleep.
His black slippers tap at the frame.
Pharaoh-fashion, his hands
lie folded over the blue shirt at his chest.
He leans to one side. He twists
at the waist, and his head
rests quietly on the brown, soft bundle of coat.

His hat has fallen into viridian grass.

Above this man, the field
rises straight up to fringe the violet sky
with firs who are
not yet the night they will soon be
as they stand
dense and bristled, looming to guard
the birch, the horse, the fence, the white pig, and
the gently lapsing shack.

All is quiet in the green field.
The crickets have ceased.
The peepers have ceased.
The grass is a moist and burning green
whose tiny roots
pry into humus, the earth's
black heart, to find
what pulses there.

The forest leans into the man's sleep.
It cannot
dream for itself.
The sky and meadow glow, the field extends,
the creatures nibble at the blazing sward
because

this single man sleeps here without
his hat.

Through the East Door

(. . . and hand in hand the lost will all be joined.)
for Theora Hamblett, painter, Oxford, Mississippi, 1895–1977

I

You could say she had no life, except

II

through shimmer of sweetgum, persimmon,
hickory,

> *red over yellow, two coats*
> *so each leaf shines separate*

the voice
commands: "Drop the handkerchief!" Children's
game. They stand
in a circle under the leaves.

> *I knew I should paint the children*

Hooded
trees tower, leaves haloed
in blue, grass strewn
with dabble of gold and muscadine.

> *I painted my dreams, later they called*
> *them visions*

28

Each leaf in order, on branch and on lawn,
the children moving in time

       yellow my strongest color

III

At the sorghum mill, horses plod in a ring
grinding the stalks; juice runs off to the troughs;

       fired, seethes red as sweetgum in autumn,
       the brush flickers too

Each act in its place: ashes of winter boiled
with hog grease make lye soap in April.
Simplest things holy: the churn
a grail. Cleaning day—and the pennanted yard,
quilts and coverlets crazily flap on the fence
while trees, tall fans, stand guard in the gentle field.

There they climb long steep Hamblett Hill
to school in the early frost—

       an utterly vertical road,
       brother Hubert, the others, and I,
       in black, trudging in pairs—

I can still see us sigh as we started
up that high hill to the maple blaze
at the crown

There was always a blaze at the crown.

IV

Haywagon crosses a ford:

river vertical,
trees a smoked olivey green

The hay with the children slides off, old Dan
stands up on the single-tree, wavers, falls,
white head smacking river rock while
the mules strain forward.

He said
he just knew we were hurt. We were not.

About three weeks later he died

In the picture, old Dan
seems to perch on his head as a trick, feet tangled
in reins, as Hubert stands by him, the little girls sit
in the fallen hay, and the river
runs past, ashen blue, as soft

as the sky, and the straight-legged mules
keep walking.

V

Who could say
she had no life, when there were
angels. The first
was Poppa, seven years dead,

> *appears at the ironing board*
> *as the irons heat up at the hearth—*
> *"No, Baby, for my sake, don't go*
> *to the ball game with Hubert. Stay home*
> *and help Mama—" flapping his sleeves*
> *and wings*

She stayed
home with Mama. She painted.

For years. Years, painted: "Heaven's Descent
to Earth," "God's Cavalry," "Shadrach, Meshach,
and Abed-Nego," "The Calamus Vine," and so
many others. Her Mama
died, she painted
alone. Salvaging, salvaging,
thronging the house.

　　　　　When Hubert
was dying, his wife
called to say he was better.

　　　　　I saw
　　　　　him come in my room
　　　　　through the east door. I knew what that meant,
　　　　　his eyes blazing round with that light—

That light, light of persimmon, sweetgum, hickory,
light of the fire on hog-killing day,
light of stacked hay, of Dan's white hair
in blood, light of new sorghum, the Golden Gate,
and chariots low out of heaven, light
of children dancing hand in hand in a ring.

　　　　　I knew
　　　　　and I cried. Hubert had become
　　　　　a part of the whole world

　　　　　I was painting all my life long

　　　　　and I knew I would paint
　　　　　him too, at the east door of the workroom,
　　　　　with those eyes,
　　　　　though I was so old already, my hands
　　　　　　　would shake.

TWO

To Max Jacob

You *were* a moral dandy, sir. The font
could have twinkled with eau-de-cologne
for all you cared; the point
was only the soul's toilette, to keep
malicious Max immaculate. The stone
on which you knelt was bare,
the walls you prayed to innocent
of any devil's ornament. And yet
your piety is touching, though
(because?) histrionic: grown
old with the actor, the gesture must
approach perfection of artifice.
Superbly you litter your skull with dust,
raise up trembling lips to kiss
the godly Host. You've scarce a hair
but yank what you can, by God,
right out at the roots.
A fourteen-year scenario
of Job on ash heap, vile,
repentant, all the while
so deadly bored you write your friends,
"The quality of work depends
all, on the *kind* of boredom."
What interior desert did you fear
so terribly, you chose
a monk's cell, not the city, for your stage?
And for your major prop, the rose
of Christ, and not of Baudelaire?

Max Jacob at Saint Benoît

The noonday square. Plane leaves, dust:
they scurry in heat shimmering gusts.
Even shadows rustle. The Belgians are gone.
The tiny terrier trots alone.
Max prayed here, *le grand poseur,*
salon mystic and *littérateur,*
but fourteen years, remember, that's one hell
of a pose for a Paris swell.
He had an infallible sense of scene.
See that stone soul torn limb from limb
between the devils and seraphim?
Romanesque, of course, for Max to preen
his own soul's pretty plumage here
year after tiresome dusty year.
And still, it wasn't easy. *Quel ennui!*
This flat, hot land, the sluggish Loire;
daily, nightly, daily: *prière, devoir;*
no more blue-yellow visions of Christ on the tree
(from Max's aquarelle), no more *cinémathèque*
blue movie Maries scolding *"pauvre Max"*
(to scandalize confessors),
no more dandified mystics dogging his tracks.
At Saint Benoît, just dust. The trek
to God? Beyond the crypt, it led
from boredom to boredom to prison camp bed
in Drancy. There, the Nazis let him die
—an old Jew with pneumonia—"naturally."

Drowned Son

I, too, have a voice.
You didn't know it?
You didn't know it
twenty-three years of my life
in the brown house
with faded prints of birds, old
novels, sepia photos of
elders with hats by the brown house.
My aunt planted flowers.
She thought
she could conquer the house.
And certain days it appeared
nasturtiums *would* shout down the walls,
delphinium flared,
fleas leapt in the lilacs,
fireweed burned in the meadow, but
not loud enough, their tongues
of flame, for always strong
faces of our living dead
with my skull, speaking, leaned,
and the truly dead went hollering
alive down our long halls at night.

But you
I could not hear. And what
could you say to me, your only son?
The path
led through spruces, earth red
with needles, twigs, flesh of wood rot;

lichen a slime green glow on bark.
It was late summer. All
I heard was the dull boom
of breakers on basalt,
far off, beyond angled and half-crashed trees.
I walked
in their blackness.
By moss, boulders storm-tossed, driftwood, to
air, wing-torn, gull-mourned, breathtaking in
greatness of gray gulf space:
                                        whereat
in the sea I seized my voice.

Strindberg in Baltimore

(after reading Strindberg's play "Easter")

If she wanders in holding a daffodil,
do not be afraid. She is not violent.
She returns home for Easter in the play
still in clinic dress, and without permission.
Escaped. But don't draw back.
If she's stolen the flower—and, in a way, she has—
it is a sign of the light she will cast in her house
where they sit, her family, numbed in shame
except for the father, shameless, in prison.

And this is the way she climbs
these shabby, Baltimore stairs into my room.

She does not scream, gibber, scratch her face.
"One does not talk of the dead,"
she says, meaning herself. But tells me that she can see
constellations in daylight, and understand
the conversations of birds. "This is not Sweden,"
I say. "Not 1900." I point
out the window to Homestead Street, where day
drains into day without
the benefit of the clerical scheme of time.
She's fading. Already Strindberg
calls her back: he's cracking up, he thinks
she will heal him. The shopkeeper finds
her misplaced coin, suspends prosecution
for the crime of the flower. Lindkvist the Creditor
turns agent of mercy. Kristina
will marry Elis. The calendar swims:

39

its pages loosed from brass rings
drift in sunlight to the floor.
All this between
Maundy Thursday and the Eve of Easter.

Elisabeth, Strindberg's sister, goes
into the asylum, where she won't get well.
And here, on Homestead Street,
no Lindkvist turns savior, nor does a sick child
appear with chalice blossom to save the day.
The Mongoloid girl
in the pink shirt arranges from morning till night
her little pile of sticks on the front porch.
God knows what she sees, but the sun
scrubs clean her round, raptly attentive face.
The gangling boy from a different
house each morning staggers three
blocks to the store, propped on his Mom.
He idiotic, she lame. It takes
from 7:15 till 9 for them to achieve
this rite, which each day demands again.

It's not unity of action I observe
from this window, but
a continuum of small gestures:
the quart of milk, the carton of eggs to be bought.
Always those twigs to be restacked.

And yet it seems
that Eleonora
would know these speechless children.
"Have you noticed,"
Strindberg has her ask, "that the only place
the nightingales sing is there, in the garden
of the Deaf and Dumb?"

Interior at Petworth: From Turner

(Lord Egremont speaks)

It was a way of punishing the house, setting it ablaze
in ruddy, golden flames; smoke
in billows up the front stairs; walls
cringing like leaves.
I say, I am afraid
in my own house. Do not believe
I started this, it was
that man, who was to portray the park alone, mind you,
but then became
enamored of the music room.
And now what have we: floods
of fire rolling from room to room, furniture wrecked
in seethe, my wife
Lady Amelia turned
wraith, God knows what fish
and drowning slaves cast up in the tide
along with pocket Bibles, snuffboxes, antimacassars, the
familiar bric-a-brac of the well-kept house.
Where are Edward, Lavinia, Jane? Why
is no one crying, "Fire! Fire!"? Am I
alone?
       The man has no sense of proportion.
He had himself lashed to the mast, once, it is said,
on a steamboat off the harbor mouth
in full blizzard: sailors blinded by snow, the boat
crippled, led by the lead, they damn near died to a man,
    and he—
he was observing "the light at sea," he said.

The painting? "Soapsuds and whitewash,"
the critics described it so.

But here, in our house, it is catastrophe
of flame, not weather, he loosed.
He is a man
in love with last things, clearly,
the last things, but
never understood the first, it seems to me,
and certainly not the genial *medias res*
of decorous, daily life.
What tea-times we've known in these chambers,
    what sonatinas,
lieder of an evening, whist,
Emmeline embroidering, the hounds calm at the hearth,
    now all
dissolved.
                Perhaps there are no flames.
A bloody haze arises, it could be
my own eyes that fail.
I hear nothing, but fear
the upstairs rooms, cramped rooms
I have not entered in ages, only remember
the draughts, creakings, grime in closet corners,
windows too tight to lean from, the smell
of antique damp. And now, who knows
what acts unroll
on narrow beds, on floorboards warped askew?

43

As steam is rising, rising? As heat
buoys the house up into an atmosphere
all of its own creation?
Who are
the participants? Where has Amelia gone?
Why, in this furnace, can I hear no sound,
or feel my own skin begin to peel?

Music for Railroad, Telephone Wire, and Easter

Compose by shadow and chrome. You will have
the land in unquenchable dying,
lines of desire strung along the tracks
uncounted miles upon whose nerve-taut wire
obsessive, the suite pursues
one murderous hum past slag heap, over marsh
pylon to pylon, by
windows, barrels, smokestacks, trestles, tanks,
flame-spurt and smoke-meander fraying form:
all solids melt
in death by multiplication, life
by reflection in the sunstruck ditch,
burnt water, harbor, oil spill, puddle, and
in bottle graveyard tumbled down a bank—
one continental cataract of trash
through which weeds thrust, not green;
and over which, in dark and lazing loops,
the hawk, in solitude, floats.
                              He scans
an Easter music from a score in flame.

Snow Day

I have nothing to say on a white afternoon
but there are the candlesticks, etched,
hieratic, guarding the pane
with arching wicks; and there is the bottle of glue, and there
squirming upward, one black curlycue
succeeding another, the jungle plant on the window sill.
The life in this room is still.
There is nothing, nothing to do
about tonnage of snow in New
Haven, or
bells that won't ring downstairs at the door
or bells, in the tower, that will.
Nothing to say, except here,
discretely, we are
shaped in the dark in a darkening room
against the snow window, against the snow day.
                                                    And I think

of my friend, who was
not really my friend,
except for the death in her eyes, which were round
and wise like a turtle's.
I think of my friend and the snow, because
of that blank haven she found
when the Buick spun into her last snow day
on Route whatever-it-was, toward nightfall, and she
had no way to say what it was that she knew
with glass in her eyes and her mouth full of snow.

Renoir

for Donald Davie

Under striped flutter of awnings, they have come
together this afternoon to glitter with
carafes and wine glasses, and the fluffy dog
perched on the table amid parings
of apples and peaches. They rehearse
a civilization here among
bright collaborations of sun. The two
gentlemen nearest us take their ease
bare-armed, in undershirts. At the next
table, brown jacket and bowler melt
into ingenious dapple and nonchalance,
and only the farthest gentlemen, vertical, sustain
in suits and top hats, a dark
decorum. And ladies, ladies—
bonnetted, buttoned at neck
and wrists, yet ripe
with sleep: their cheeks
and half-closed eyes give them away.
Flesh is fruit, whispers the brush, and sunlight
wine; all cloth
dissolves. And when these chroma
and characters have faded
into the single, sensual blur of an afternoon
lost, there will remain
ghostly vermilion, hieroglyphic lips,
awning stripes and anemones that once
so vulgarly blazed, now dimming to
the mystic map of sprawl, spatter, and glare:

not Jeanne, Marie-Thérèse, Alphonse, Auguste, but this—
this truest pattern, radiance revealed,
a constellation visible at dusk.

Water Lily

The highway forever draws away
day and night in a whine and purr of trucks,
and your face recedes, as time
accumulates between us,

but I remember one morning when we lay
together on a flat rock
in a brown, unwinding stream
and the sun spread gloss

across the water. Sparrows came
to dabble in the shallows. A stray cloud
shadowed us, vanished,
shadowed us again

and in the fluttered light we were the same
as stone and ripple. Water played out loud
twisting in harness;
one leaf ran

swivelling down the current, green canoe
sidetracked in eddies, released, then lost
for good. In this strange
space we invent

separately day by day between us, you
can't hear me breathing, touch me, taste
the sun's change
on my cheek; can't

hold me, tell me to hush. The wasps crawl
over their paper palace cell by cell
where pupae sleep
and swell toward their brief

flight and the end of summer. Wind riffles tall
pines' sleeves. Beyond, the highway still
trails away, but deep
in its own life

the pond lies motionless. From frog scum
and ragged clouds, the lily blooms,
a white-fleshed star
with dab of sun at heart.

It holds its peace against the tire's hum,
hot miles of fleeing where the asphalt screams,
summer uncoiling in which we are
farther and farther apart.

Antietam Creek

(22,000 *dead: September 17, 1862*)

The lovers cross the bridge, and the brown stream
slides along rusting fields. The lovers hear
papyrus shush of cornstalks as they climb
the hill, and a crow calling. October air

burns auburn. High, a hawk
laces the sky. The slow blood crawls
up pokeweed, bright pink in the stalk
to blurt black in the berries. The couple strolls

the hillcrest now, hand held in hand, as though
Sumner had never slashed through Bloody Lane
nor Hill's mistaken "About face" split his ranks

while Burnside fumbled. The lovers read no
bronze plaques bolted to granite. They will drink wine,
make love in the fluvial field by crumbling banks,

till evening drains the landscape, and they go
hand gripping hand, coats buttoned, heads held low.

51

"Ille mi par . . ."

(Catullus LI, from Sappho)

He's like a god, that man; he seems
(if this can be) to shine beyond
the gods, who nestling near you sees
   you and hears you

laughing low in your throat. It tears me
apart. For when I glimpse you,
Lesbia, look—I'm helpless:
   tongue a frozen

lump, and palest fire
pouring through all my limbs; my ears
deafened in ringing; each eye
   shuttered in night.

. . . . .
You're wasting your time, Catullus,
laying waste to your life. You love it.
Whole kingdoms and blissful cities
   have wasted away, like you.

Catullus XI

Furius and Aurelius, you fine friends
of Catullus, whether he forces his way
to farthest India where the Eastern shore
    unrolls, booming in surf;

whether he trudges among Hyrcanians, languid
Arabs, Scythians, Parthian bowmen, or
along that delta stained by the seven
    mouths of the Nile;

whether he marches clear over the Alps and there
surveys great Caesar's dominions,
the Gallic Rhine, and savage, far-off, un-
    imaginable Britons—

you who would traipse with your dear friend all
over the world, wherever the gods' design
might call, just take to my darling
    this little message:

let her live, let her flourish, with all her lovers,
let her seize in her cunt three hundred at a time
loving none, but time and again exploding
    their bloated members.

But she'd better not look, like last time, for my
love reviving. It's her fault it's fallen,
at flower at the rim of the meadow, touched
    by the plow passing.

Embrace

Outside, in moonlight,
boughs clutch at night, roots grapple rock and frozen dirt.
I lie in bed awake;
hold the pewter gleam
of darkness close;
hear wind finger the trees,
sift through stiff marsh grass, thickets, loose
boards in barns, protruding eaves,
seek and seek and leave only the wheeze of its passing.

In summer, a moment clasped us,
its only motion a waver
in the tall, plumed tips of pines.
We believed in our bodies, as we believe in words
while the pen moves.

At the station stairs, shoulders already hunched
into a future of departures,
you turned, and looked back once.
"Call," you said, and descended,
where so many trains had drawn away
and a new one, now, was slowly easing in.

Street

You walked out into a morning torn
apart in the throats of dogs, and under sharp
brittle leaves—the whole seam
of the street opened to let the air
of autumn in, and you
out, into the clarity of being alone, where even
the frills of birdsong had been drawn aside.
Each house was still blinded in sleep, its peaked
hat tucked firmly around the eaves.
Hedges hugged the yards, cozy as winter collars.
Parked cars hemmed the sidewalk, predictable as
teeth on a zipper. But you moved down
the central gash toward where the last dawn blue
drained free at the vanishing point.
As you walked, you heard
mutts and shepherds lunging at wire fences,
thudded back at the chest, and flinging again.
But you kept on, and the taste
of light was liquor distilled
new, pure, tongue-slicing, yours alone.

Invitation au Voyage: Baltimore

Egyptian freighter, whining Arabic tunes,
muddy coffee over the galley flame . . .

What explorers we are, testing the gangplank
of someone else's ship.

On the wharf, Helen's Bar:
she's welcomed sailors in
for fifty years, manning the counter alone, upright

as a new bottle. Dog asleep
in a rocker, jukebox fat as a pope. Enter the swain
bearing his nightly gardenia, for her,

for her brandy glass.
We travel back
to my frostbitten garden, where you try

to harvest gourds by moonlight, filling the alley
with arias, you're that drunk

and in love
with the impossible, I'm that drunk
and in love with some

idea of you, revenant
from another century:

when we turn to kiss,
the whole sea swarms between us.

An abyss.

Virgin Pictured in Profile

for Ariel and Huxley Miller

A white-gowned woman making offering
rests on one knee, the other raised.
Hands outstretched, palms down,
fingers slightly curved at the tips.
Spine a straight stem. The visible ear
left bare by the black, geometric coiffure.

Where does she gaze with that slant, blank eye?
The amphora before her is empty.
So are the bowl and narrow vase.
She kneels, rigid in ceremony.
No one stands near her,
and the world beyond is milk mist only.

They have gone: maidens, parents, the robed priest,
the people of her town, even the gods.
So rapt she was
in the rite, she did not hear
when they called and trundled away.
Beams crumbled on sand and shards, and wind
curled in from the desert.

She did not hear, nor will she ever.
"Child, child, wake up," they had cried,
but could not break her trance, and so
departed, with all their belongings
wrapped in bright woven cloth, their dogs at their heels.

They died. Somewhere, the river rises still,
fish feed, and fields are tilled,
the newly dead are laid in the living earth.
Of this she will never know.
It is the perfection of emptiness
she offers now, as she offered long ago.

No river rises to her wall,
mud-roiled, flooding with spring.
Her landscape is pure dust.
Nor will it be granted
to her who never soiled her loins with life
to enter, lotus in hand, and dressed as bride,
the full-thronged kingdom of the truly dead.

THREE

Jigsaw Puzzle in the Suburbs

for Stephen

While you assemble Monte Carlo
piece by blue-gray piece, encouraging
the small, stump-limbed
fragments to snuggle

logically, the teen-aged
girls upstairs
bawl, shredding
their voices at each other

and the toddler next door
meanders unsteadily across our plot
of basil and young tomatoes.
I share the room

as you pore
over the linkage of smoke-green hills, stacked
terraces, ashen
foreign streets; I try

to conjugate
from memory the Greek verb
"to learn," and the child
in my womb gently nudges me on.

Our other neighbor, Lou,
paces his porch, growling
at Jews, his banged-up Buick, and maple boughs
that snatch at his hat:

I'm learning
that Lou is real; in fact,
smiling his bristly
smile, gave us the puzzle. In Monte

Carlo, a gem-blue rectangle
starts to emerge: public pool.
Those cobwebs
must be rigging

of yachts, I say. We fought
last night, not knowing
why, but lying awake
hours, apart,

then sleeping stiffly, to wake up
ignorant
in each other's arms.
In the puzzle, two more

blues lock. It is all
starting to fit: this picture
we piece together
while our child

grows toward us, quivering
in darkness with wide open eyes. More
shrieks from upstairs, already
heard in the womb.

64

The child can't see, but will learn,
how you've found
a conjugation of shadows for the heart
of the harbor;

and how, for a moment, we rest there while
this day, like the young
basil, rises into late afternoon
in spite of us all.

Child's Room in Autumn

The scene is about order, the maple tree
a conflagration trapped in the rectangle
of window, the Newton High football
players outside an explosion surging free

of the grip of game and field.
And the sky is gray cotton
batting pressing down
over us, wadded by skilled

hands between branches and rooflines.
October wants to ignite.
In Benjamin's room, a set
of toy soldiers shines

along the shelf, jumble
of prancing eras
armed with bazookas, crossbows, spears.
Tacked to the wall,

a *Map of Planet
Earth's Disaster Areas* shows
garlands of volcanoes
spilling cherries out

to sea, buttercups for
earthquakes, a lime-green swarm
of bees the tornado alarm:
toy translations of war

sprinkled across the map
as though catastrophe were a board game
you could win. The room
holds peace in a trap

of representations. Ben's at school,
the house clenches its calm,
the *Times* softly delivers its daily harm
in grisaille blur, but geometrical:

pyramid-hunched, a mother grieves
over small bodies arranged in a row;
elsewhere, a darkhaired boy
stands alone as the last jeep leaves

under a charred, rectangular swatch of sky.
The scenes are about
suffering, how it lurches out
of any picture, giving the lie

to pity, to composition.
I sweep Benjy's room,
waiting for him to come
home, happy with stories: he'll run

out into the autumn field
where, now,
cheers erupt, helmets are tossed high,
and leaves swim down in wild

shoals, gold pennants, streamers
loosened to glorify
the field, the ephemeral victors,
leaving the boughs to the sky.

Couple

(for Isabel Archer)

You turn to the window, and whatever it was
we were discussing escapes
in a flutter of poplar leaves:
we are left with mere afternoon, in a daze,

aging, but still taking notes, while
the fritillary summer flaps
from the laundry line, and bell tolls blossom
in air, floating in from the tawniest hill.

I boiled months
of sunlight, trapped them in jars
of apricot jam. Where were
you last night, where was I? Who counts

the slashes? We take
our time. This life
in the villa continues
behind high glass-fringed walls, smoke

drifting in from the fields, letters
arriving torn, Antiquity
more legible than our own
dear pasts. With gin and bitters

and years, we'll understand, how comprehensible
our magics will have become, how tuned
to our garden where such lush symbols thrive.
We'll be a story, we'll be able

to parse it alone in crepuscular light,
so pleased, hearing distant bleats of horns
from every blind loop of the road as small
cars accelerate into the future, trusting not

to collide, each with its destined mate.

The Back Yards

Listen, it's coming, the calm
after the rain.
To all the back yards of our alley,
past the stadium, up to Druid Park,
it's coming, the quieting down.

The zinnias straining on strings
tied to the iron pipe, give in.
Accept to be leashed, held half-erect.
The fig tree shudders, nods.
Dell and Diane, from over the wire fence,
have stolen the last few fruits.
The rest are fallen, squashed.
The boughs accept.

And Mrs. Dunbar's laundry,
drenched again, receives the small wind:
T-shirts, dungarees, dishtowels
motion casually from the line
as if further comment were useless.

Oak leaves lie
on raggedy grass, on asphalt,
lapped one over the other,
hand-splayed, mingled, still.
Finally quiet, they gleam
in evening light,
wet, dark salmon-tinted
and Naples yellow.

Even the dogs have stopped
their ruckus. Have gone indoors,
shaking out droplets from fur, and last growls.
And only trashcans now stand guard,
erratically placed, at the gates of the wire fences,
over the new peace
that has settled down to inhabit the back yards

with you not here to see them.

"Funere Mersit Acerbo"

(Carducci)

You, asleep up there on the flowering
Tuscan hill, lying beside your father,
among the graveyard grasses, didn't you hear
just now a tender voice weeping?

It's my child, my little boy, who knocks at your lonely
door, he in whose holy name
you lived again. Life fled from him
also, brother, life so bitter for you.

He was playing among bright flower-
beds, laughing at light-hearted fancies, when
the shadow wrapped him round, and shoved him to your

solitary shores. O, down
in the darkness, welcome him, since he's small
and turns to the sunlight, calling his mother still.

Rocamadour

Light traces merely the rims of stone steps
so that we shall ascend on shadow, past slanting walls
to narrower stairs worn down by years
of feet pressing to climb.
The virgin we've come to see,
black, ivory, curved like a drawn bow,
could be standing in any one
of a number of rooms.
We'll each seek her alone.
But we linger here
where the lemon tree spouting up from a hidden court
spreads boughs arrested in shower above our heads.

The town
appears empty of people. Yet, somone has hung
two gray, fraying washrags out to dry
from a window sill up ahead,
and further still, a cracked clay pot
foists its single geranium on the scene.
Sturdy, gawky, unrepentantly red:
clearly well-watered.
                              We have come to see this statue
of no particular beauty, except it is said
for centuries she compelled
the vows of pilgrims who climbed these steps on their knees.
We too have come
for years, it seems, circuitously toward her who,
for all we know, no longer even stands
in this silent town. Not that we knew

when we hiked the vineyards of Nuits St. Georges
past villages decked in paper flowers, where even
toddlers reeled cockeyed drunk, that it was she
who drew us. Drew us beyond the grove
in which oaks circled no dragon, but simply a worm
in a pool of rain. Drew us beyond
cafés, highways, gas stations, gardens, nights,
dim apartments, dingy plants,
silences, sunlight on water, on ruined stone,
till here we stand,
not knowing quite how we have come
or where we are, with mountains strewn behind
like boulders on sand beneath this citadel.

We stand at the foot of the stairs.
The shadow lengthens from the courtyard wall
across the cobbles, blurring edges of steps
where we will walk.
Give me your hand.
We have come this far
together, apart. She waits in an inner room
toward which we will climb in twilight. The lemon tree
gathers sleep in its branches, ravels it there.

It is time to go in.

Visitation

I

The pieties could be, she thought, discarded.
It was to be a day, a long day, the kind
when plum wine rises in the glass
of its own accord, and coffee gives off
the warm, dark odor of possibility.
The dictionary had not tuned her for the future,
but a man walked in
crying where oh where is my lost love
and released six gray doves from his hat.

A June landscape ripens in dappled light.
On blond fields, beyond cedars, ponies graze.
Honeysuckle trails in the lane. But so
unseasonably cold!
                    That night
It was the story flung from burning logs,
all red and gold, that broke into the house
of sleep, and, ravisher, revealed them both.

II

I remember, in earliest morning, how light cracks
along edges of trees. Roses sway
under its impact, loosing red petals and white
to curl and turn slowly brown on new-mown grass.

The petals lie, all day, turning and turning
into their futures under the influence of that light.

I couldn't touch you. You couldn't forgive.

In any event the mist burned off the fields,
rising and disappearing into fine-spun blue.
By eleven that morning we walked
up the road into a pool of pure sun
where hewn stones survived from a previous age.

Happiness arrived apace in strange forms
over dense, copper-green hills,
pranced in among the roses and as quickly fled.
Unease among the oaks: massed leaves stirred
high from their hush, sheltered birds trilled
in cool and quickening air. I thought
that warbling might have saved us.
I was wrong.

Realm of visitation. Realm of denial.
To which did we belong?
You prophesied in ashes,
but I, my mind astray, refused to hear;
merely watched the ponies move from the shade of boughs
into patches of yellow, and back, while the locust tree
rained honey, and bees shrouded the leaves in veils of song.

Pastorale

*("There is no Time in the Spirit, but there is a time
for man. This is one of the keys." André Derain)*

Waking to fern leaf that, printed in brain shale,
a single night, stream-murmurous, had pressed
from sleep, he wandered across damp grass.
Fingered the fossil of dream. Thought:
I have come back.

He had come back.

Released
from the City of Selves, he found
the tangle, arthritic, of the apple tree,
braided brook, pale root prying soil,
day sopped with fog, owl hoot at night:
moments so slowly elided he could not tell
where slippage occurred, except
that once again it was dawn,
once again it was night.

Caught in the larger dying
he saw no instant blaze aloud to truth.
But as the berry gathers blue
slow to the small, smooth orb in the leaf's shadow,
and as the apple aches to fulfill the sphere,
so each moment swelled, and he sensed it grow,
and only brook song filled his ear.

And now? Time in his blood, he turned
back to the windowed world, its human hours.
Miraculous, though, the faces he had known,

now that in their eyes he saw
the stream's gold flecks, and in their voices heard,
beneath their words, its deliquescence, golden, flow.

Orchard

in memoriam W.K.

Crippled by years of pruning, the apple branch
bends toward me, and I pick
the wizened, fiery fruit you offered years
ago, as you were dying.

Years, it took, for the fact
of your simply not
answering to ripen
within me. Only now

as I sit, pregnant, marooned
in tall grass, cross-hatched
by October sunlight, with the *thunk*
of apples falling, can I taste

your absence. Pale
green, acidic. A spurt
of saliva quickens the mouth.
From the lower field

float yelps and laughter
of children tussling among
hummocks. Their fathers grope
higher into the branches, hands

stretching to grasp
that flecked, streaked
russets and McIntosh. Those men
are woven into a basketwork of boughs

80

and I am heavy on the ground below
surrounded
by bruised fruit and a fermenting
glow that rises

as apple haze from the weeds.
You had no children.
But you gave
me a painting of apples

shrivelled and burning,
which I remember now
and again, so that I may
learn, as you did, how

passionately to die. In
time, in time. My child
stirring within me weighs me down.
You have come

to meet us through
the braided seasons, and I see
how, rusting and golden, already
we are following you.

"Sea Gate and Goldenrod"

(Cranberry Island Elegy)

for W.K.

Feather damp white with a whiff of putrefaction,
spruces ink green, how gray dissolves
a doorway after three straight weeks
of fog: you took it all

to heart. Your house,
anchored on rock, but hung
with flags, wanted
to sail. Light, when it appears

in a white, Maine room
has an edge
keen enough to slice
the hand, and you offered

your hands. Across
the road, beyond black woods, the sea
kept slurring the same
day in, day out.

You listened, leaning
back in bed, the world
a patchwork map spread out
over your failed legs.

You knew, you connoisseur.
On our
island, alders shimmied in sunlight, deer
browsed through cranberry bogs.

But there are
other islands, and already, while we sat
here with you chatting of ours with its goldenrod,
what you heard

was the other islands.

In a Tuscan Landscape

       A web
floats over the morning, and we are held
       here by the ply
of voice within laughing voices, butterfly

       scripture, linden
air embroidered in birdsong, and, most
       visibly, by
smoke unwinding from burnt stubble to laze

       across vineyards. How
long can we be held? The child so steeped
       in dream her very
flesh seems sleep incarnate, already clenches

       puckering, dimpled
fists. Yet here, we imagine, is peace
       perfected, daze
in which tractor buzz and rooster have been

       tamed, and the same
rusting earth which nurses the vines will take
       us and wrap
us carefully in cypress roots at the end.

       But
something else in us cries
       out, breaking
the rhythm, inquisitorial, schooled in the

84

        arts of
pain, so that we throng the summer exhibition
            Atroci
Macchine della Tortura nella Storia, gaily

        advertised on
pennants in the city streets. Even
            the tractor
harrows the field as though searching

        for knowledge. That smoke
from scorched earth is a bandage which never will staunch
        our ingenious hurts, or heal
those wounds my daughter's sleep can't yet imagine.

Painting a Madonna

If he has been so careful
in drawing the jointure of wrist and still child-like hand
            it is because
he himself does not quite believe

            in the spirit.
And yet, what else could account
            for the pale
dome of her brow, for flesh so fragile that

            it yearns toward
translucence like the veil which floats
            over her
calligraphic curls? He could almost see

            the Incarnation
as a trick of light. And maybe
            it was, radiance
so preoccupying her body she gave birth to

            its source. Still,
pigment is mineral, canvas is woven
            thread, the painter's
hand, as it moves, a machine of muscle and bone.

            Our daughter finds
she, too, has fingers, fingers! and grasps
            at grass, closing,
unclosing tiny, definite, fists, stained green.

86

Around us, the garden
labors: the vine surges into the grapes, the tree
        bows over as if
worshiping its own pears, a column of ants

        minutely dismembers
the fledgling fallen among weeds. Our air
        drowses in scents
of linden, lavender, decay. Like Thomas,

        we have
to touch to believe. So the madonna, bent
        over her sleeping
child, strokes with one finger the insect bite marring

        His brow. She is watching
Him die. And now, for the first time, feels
        her own death stir
like a second child within her, and love, which we call the
        soul.

Notes

"Funerary Portraits"
Hellenistic Period, bas-relief.

"Omalos"
A village in a mountain plateau in Crete. The name means "level," hence "ordinary."

"Haoma"
In Persian mythology, Haoma is a tree of eternal life.

"To Max Jacob" and "Max Jacob at Saint Benoît"
Max Jacob (1876–1944) was a Jewish painter and poet, close companion to Picasso, Apollinaire, and Derain. He converted to Catholicism (with Picasso as his improbable godfather) and spent his last years in the monastery of St. Benoît. In 1944 the Nazis discovered him there and seized him as he was helping to celebrate mass. His friend Cocteau tried to arrange his release, but he died of pneumonia in the German camp at Drancy before permission came through.

"Interior at Petworth: From Turner"
Turner painted a series of paintings for his patron, Lord Egremont, between 1830 and 1837. Some were interiors from Lord Egremont's own house, Petworth. I have taken liberties with the historical character of Lord Egremont.

"Virgin Painted in Profile"
Egyptian fresco, Middle Kingdom, from the Walters Art Gallery, Baltimore.